Miss Hazeltine's Home for Shy and Fearful Cats

by Alicia Potter · illustrated by Birgitta Sif

Alfred A. Knopf · New York

THIS IS A BORZOI BOOK PUBLISHED BY ALFRED A. KNOPF

Visit us on the Web! randomhouse.com/kids
Educators and librarians, for a variety of teaching tools, visit us at
RHTeachersLibrarians.com

Library of Congress Cataloging-in-Publication Data
Potter, Alicia.
Miss Hazeltine's Home for Shy and Fearful Cats / written by Alicia Potter ; illustrated by Birgitta Sif.—First edition.
p. cm.
Summary: Miss Hazeltine opens her home to cats who need help learning how to be brave,
and their new skills are put to use when she finds herself in a bind.
ISBN 978-0-385-75334-0 (trade) — ISBN 978-0-385-75335-7 (lib. bdg.) — ISBN 978-0-385-75336-4 (ebook)
[1. Cats—Fiction. 2. Fear—Fiction.] I. Sif, Birgitta, illustrator. II. Title.
PZ7.P847Mi 2015
[E]—dc23
2013031961

The text of this book is set in 19-point Perpetua Regular.
The illustrations were hand drawn in pencil and colored digitally.

MANUFACTURED IN CHINA
May 2015
10 9 8 7 6 5 4 3 2 1

First Edition

To my feral foster kittens,
who inspired this story,
and to Yodel, who stayed
—A.P.

To my purr-fect little girls,
Sóley and Salka
—B.S.

When Miss Hazeltine opened her Home for Shy and Fearful Cats, she didn't know if anyone would come.

Miss Hazeltine's Home for Shy and Fearful Cats

But come they did.

"He runs from mice!"

"She's scared of birds!"

"Can't pounce!"

"Won't purr!"

"Hopeless!"

"Worthless!"

"Afraid of EVERYTHING!"

Strays who could read Miss Hazeltine's
sign skittered in on their own.
 Then there was Crumb, the most timid
of all. He dashed through the door . . .

. . . and hid.

Miss Hazeltine began her
lessons at once.
In the morning, she
taught Bird Basics.

In the afternoon,
Climbing Up, followed
by Climbing Down.

At night was Scary Noises.

Many cats received extra help
in Meeting New Friends.

Miss Hazeltine showed the
cats how to hold their tails
high. To arch their backs.
To think good thoughts.

Every day, they
practiced pouncing.

The hardest lesson?
How Not to Fear the Broom.

Miss Hazeltine didn't mind if some cats only watched. She let them be.

Like Crumb.

Miss Hazeltine told him that, sometimes, she got scared.

"I'm afraid of mushrooms and owls," she confided. "And I've never liked the dark."

She praised Crumb's love of pitch-black places.

Crumb lapped up every word. One day he
hoped to find the courage to thank her.
Still, he worried. Would he ever be brave?

Soon more cats came to Miss Hazeltine's home. And
more. And more.

So many arrived that on a Monday at five o'clock, when
everyone but Crumb was fast asleep, Miss Hazeltine ran out
of milk.

"I'm off to fetch a bucketful," she told Crumb, "and will
be back before dark."

Crumb watched her go.

But by the time Miss Hazeltine
rounded the road back home, the sun
had set.

The heavy buckets
sloshed and slowed her,

and her ankles were wibbly-
wobbly from all the pouncing.
Miss Hazeltine tripped . . .

. . . and fell into a ditch.

With her ankle sore and
throbbing, Miss Hazeltine was
stuck. She shivered in the dark.
The pitch-black dark. Was that
an owl hooting? She peered
around. Mushrooms!

Miss Hazeltine tried to think
good thoughts.

Back home, the cats did the same.

But they were alone—
and very, very afraid.

They didn't know where
Miss Hazeltine had gone!

And they hadn't yet had the lesson on What to
Do When the Lady You Love Goes Missing.

But Crumb knew where
Miss Hazeltine had gone.

And maybe, just
maybe, what to do.

Crumb stepped
into the moonlight.

He arched his back.
He held his tail high.

He gathered the others.
Armed with nothing but the
old broom, the residents of Miss
Hazeltine's Home for Shy and
Fearful Cats streamed into the night.

Down in the ditch, Miss Hazeltine groaned.

"What will happen to the cats?" she whispered.
"And dear, dear Crumb?"

Yet something *was* happening. The
cats felt it in their chests. With Crumb
at the fore, they followed the sweet
smell of milk down the road . . .

. . . right to Miss Hazeltine!

At Crumb's meow, the cats stared down the mushrooms.

They purred
to drown out the
owl's hoots.

And they pounced to be sure nothing lurked in the dark.

Then they formed a chain of cats to rescue
Miss Hazeltine from the ditch.

The broom made an excellent crutch.

Miss Hazeltine was escorted back to the
Home for Shy and Pretty Brave If You Ask Us
Cats (as the strays amended the sign).

"You're as bold as lions!" Miss Hazeltine told her rescuers. "And whether you stay forever or head out into the world, I will never forget your courage."

The cats were so happy that they didn't even miss their milk.

Especially Crumb . . .

. . . who had found a new favorite spot.